School For Trolls

"Yes, thank you, Miss Shirley," said Coral. "I didn't realize I wouldn't be able to get down again. You see, I wanted to be like Mirabel – Mirabel's a troll."

Coral squashed her hands in front of her mouth, but it was too late.

"A troll!" said Mr Jenkins. "But Mirabel, we don't have trolls at Millbank Juniors!"

Before anyone could say another word, Mirabel ran across the play-ground, out and all the way e.

More *brilliant* Young Hippo School stories:

CLAIRE RONAN

School
For Trolls

Illustrated by Serena Feneziani

Hippo

In Loving Memory of
Louise Jocasta Clarke

Scholastic Children's Books,
Commonwealth House, 1–19 New Oxford Street,
London WC1A 1NU, UK
a division of Scholastic Ltd
London ~ New York ~ Toronto ~ Sydney ~ Auckland

First published by Scholastic Ltd, 1998

Text copyright © Claire Ronan, 1998
Illustrations copyright © Serena Feneziani, 1998

ISBN 0 590 11234 1

Typeset by T W Typesetting, Midsomer Norton, Bath, Somerset
Printed by Cox & Wyman Ltd, Reading, Berks.

Chapter 1

A New Dress

Mirabel lived in some caves near the top of a mountain with her mum, Florence.

One day, she woke up early. I'm going to start school today, she thought.

She and Mum had filled in all the forms for Millbank Juniors and written, in their best writing –

Mirabel Blueberry
1, Dragon Haven,
Misty Mountains,
Far-Side
Rocky River

There was just one problem. Mirabel hadn't told the school she was a troll.

She tiptoed into her mum's bedroom. Mum was fast asleep, snoring, her pipe still in her mouth. Her tangly blue hair was full of cobwebs and dead spiders.

"Time to get up," whispered Mirabel.

Mum grunted and opened eyes as big as two blue china teacups. She sat up in her straw bed, lit her pipe and puffed clouds of green smoke around the cave.

"I wish you'd stop smoking, Mum, it's very bad for you," said Mirabel.

Mum yawned and brushed bits of cobweb from her nightie. "Is breakfast ready yet, dear?" she said.

"I'll dig up something in the vegetable patch," said Mirabel.

She hurried outside to the vegetable patch and dug up fifteen turnips, as knobbly as old knees. Then she climbed up the apple tree and picked Mum an apple, as red and shiny as a cricket ball.

Indoors, she plopped the turnips into the cooking pot. Soon, a thick turnip stew bubbled.

Mum lumbered into the kitchen.

She poured herself a bowl of stew and drained it in one gulp.

"I've picked you an apple, Mum," said Mirabel.

Mum bit an enormous lump from the apple. "Delicious!" she mumbled, with little pieces of apple shaking in her beard. "You know, Mirabel dear, I can't remember anything I've forgotten and yet I'm sure there's something I'm supposed to remember today. Is it your birthday?"

"No, Mum!" groaned Mirabel. "That was three months ago! Today's the day I start at my new school in the city."

"That's it," said Mum, then her chin wobbled like a jelly. "Oh, I'm going to miss you today, dear. It's not too late to change your mind and stay at home. I've taught you how to write and read and everything you need to know about being a troll."

"But Mum, there's all sorts of other things I need to know. Things like spelling and adding and taking away again."

"You know how to build a tree house, how to milk a goat and how to make a lovely cup of nettle tea," said Mum.

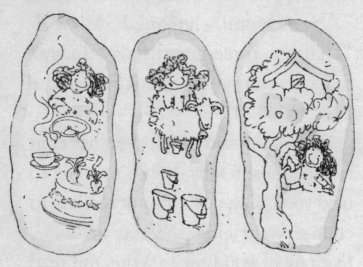

"But I need to make friends too— there aren't any other trolls around here for me to play with."

"You're right, dear," sighed Mum. Then she hurried out of the kitchen. A moment later she came back, holding up a blue, flowery dress. "Isn't it lovely?" she said. "I've sewn daisies all over it and it smells of pond water and dandelions. I made it especially for you to wear for school."

Mirabel squeezed herself inside the dress and looked at her reflection in a mirror flecked with green. The dress was a bit tight over her bottom – she'd have to be careful when she sat down. Her hair was a tangle of blue squiggles but her blue face and freckles looked clean and shiny.

Mirabel twirled around for Mum to see her new dress. "How do I look, Mum?" she said.

Mum smiled and plucked a twig out of Mirabel's hair. "You look lovely!"

Chapter 2

Off to School

Mirabel picked up her school picnic hamper. "I'll see you at home time, Mum."

Mum squashed Mirabel's packed lunch inside the hamper. "Now dear, whatever you do, don't tell anyone you're a troll or they might not want you at their school."

"Don't worry," said Mirabel.

Mum shook her head sadly and her silver pirate's earrings rattled.

Mirabel kissed her fuzzy cheek then off she went.

She squelched through the vegetable patch in her hobnail boots. On the other side, there was a jungle. Mirabel and Mum had planted trees, brambles, nettles, thistles and every kind of tangly thing they could think of. They called it their nature garden. Insects wriggled, frogs croaked, birds sang and furry animals blinked out at Mirabel with eyes like black buttons.

Mirabel wove her way through the nature garden, then she set off down the mountainside. Halfway down, she paused and looked back.

The nature garden had faded into a green smudge, no bigger than a patch on an elbow.

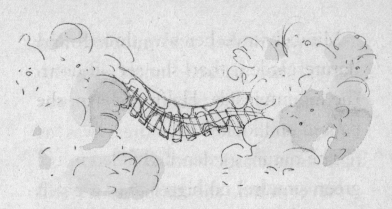

Mirabel hurried across a slatted rope bridge. Far below she saw the river glint as it threaded its way through the mountains. As soon as she reached the other side of the bridge, Mirabel flopped down on top of a rock. She peered inside her picnic hamper and pulled out some goat's cheese, turnip sandwiches, Mum's best cabbage cake and a flask of nettle tea.

"I'll have a little nibble," she said to herself, "and I'll save the rest for later."

Soon, Mirabel had nibbled and slurped her packed lunch away to nothing. As she stood up she was bursting-full. Her new dress was as tight as an elastic band.

Never mind, she thought, it's still another three miles to the school. After I've walked all that way, my dress might fit me again!

Three miles later, Mirabel reached the city. She took a small, crumpled map from her pocket and amongst the jumble of roads and houses made her way to the school. It was a concrete building with long glass windows. One very tall tree grew in the middle of the playground. A sign outside the school said –

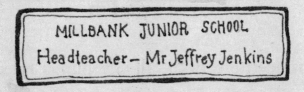

MILLBANK JUNIOR SCHOOL
Headteacher – Mr Jeffrey Jenkins

Children trailed in long crocodiles through the school gates. Mirabel's heart bumped as she followed after them.

Chapter 3

Saved by a Pin

Inside the school, all the pupils lined up in rows. They looked at Mirabel with round eyes.

I'm much bigger than the others, she thought, as she shuffled into the back row. But she had a good view over the tops of all the children's heads.

One by one, teachers marched into

the room and stood on a platform at the far end. A small man with glasses like the bottoms of jamjars climbed on to the platform. "Good morning, everybody," he said. "I am your headteacher, Mr Jeffrey Jenkins. Welcome to the new term at Millbank Juniors. Now, can any of our old pupils remember what I tell all the new pupils on their first day?"

A small girl next to Mirabel put up her hand. She had a dark face and her hair was twisted into a hundred tiny plaits, each with a coloured bead winking on the end. "I know!" she cried.

"Yes, Coral?" said Mr Jenkins.

"Is it... It's not fun, it's not cool, I don't want to go to school?"

"No, it certainly isn't," sighed Mr Jenkins. "Does anyone know the real answer?"

"I was only joking, Mr Jenkins," said Coral. "The real answer is... Read well, write well, draw well and do your sums well."

"That's it, well done!" said Mr Jenkins.

At that moment, Mirabel's socks sunk down into baggy woollen puddles around her ankles. She bent down and yanked one up. Her dress ripped. One great big rip, all the way down the back. It sounded like a ship's sails tearing.

"Are you all right in the back there? You look rather blue in the face," called Mr Jenkins.

"I ate too much breakfast," said Mirabel, "and when I bent down to pull my socks up, my dress burst. You see, my mum made me all these turnip sandwiches and baked me this delicious cabbage cake…"

The school giggled.

"I've got a safety pin she can borrow," cried Coral.

"Good," said Mr Jenkins.

"Turn around," said Coral, "and I'll pin your dress together."

Coral pinned Mirabel's dress and then looked up at her with brown button eyes. "You're a troll, aren't you?" she whispered. "I've read all about trolls in a book from our class book corner."

"Yes," whispered Mirabel. "But please don't tell."

"Is your dress firmly pinned?" said Mr Jenkins.

"Yes, thank you," said Mirabel.

"It doesn't look as if you're wearing our school uniform," said Mr Jenkins. "It looks rather like a lot of blue cobwebs and knitted seaweed. Come to my office after assembly and I'll give you a Millbank Juniors jumper and skirt."

Chapter 4

A Smart Jumper

After assembly, Coral showed Mirabel how to find Mr Jenkins' office.

Inside the office, Mr Jenkins sat behind his desk, which was piled high with books and papers. "You're new, aren't you?" he said.

"That's right," said Mirabel. "This is my first day at Millbank Juniors."

Mirabel wriggled her bottom into the seat opposite Mr Jenkins. The seat was far too small and she bulged out over the edges.

Mr Jenkins leafed through a pile of papers on his desk. "First of all, I'll check I've got your name and address. I always write a letter to all my new pupils' parents."

"You can't write to my mum," said Mirabel.

"Why not?" said Mr Jenkins.

"Because we live in a cave and we haven't got a letterbox."

Mr Jenkins chuckled. "You're good at making up stories," he said. "The next thing you'll tell me is that you sleep in a bed made of straw!"

"Yes and it's very comfy," said Mirabel.

Mr Jenkins looked puzzled. "What did you say your name was?"

"Mirabel Blueberry."

Mr Jenkins ran his finger down a sheet of paper. "Here we are … Mirabel Blueberry, 1, Dragon Haven, Misty Mountains, Far-Side, Rocky River."

"That's me," said Mirabel.

"I suppose that's the new estate that's sprung up on the other side of the motorway. They always think up wonderful names for places like that."

Mr Jenkins tapped out a number on his phone. "I'm phoning one of my teachers, Miss April Shirley, to come and meet you, Mirabel," he said. "Hello, April?" he said into the phone. "It's Mr Jenkins here, can you come to my office please?"

Mr Jenkins put down the phone. "Er ... by the way, Mirabel, I'm sorry to tell you that I don't let pupils at Millbank Juniors dye their hair blue."

"But this is my real hair," said Mirabel.

"Nobody has blue hair…" began Mr Jenkins. At that moment, a lady with long brown plaits poked her head around the door.

"Ah, April, come in and meet Mirabel," said Mr Jenkins. "Mirabel, this is Miss April Shirley, she's one of our best teachers. I've decided to put you in her class."

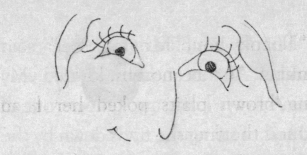

For a second, Miss Shirley's eyes widened as she looked at Mirabel, then she smiled. "Pleased to meet you, Mirabel," she said. "You'll find my classroom next door. It's class 3C. I'd better go and start taking the register – I'll see you in a moment."

Miss Shirley left the office and Mr Jenkins found Mirabel a jumper. It had "Millbank Juniors" written on the front in white letters.

"I don't think I've got a skirt in your size," said Mr Jenkins. "But you can wear this jumper over your dress for the time being."

"Thank you, Mr Jenkins," said Mirabel. "It's beautifully knitted. My mum always knits my jumpers out of old bits of string she finds down by the river, but they're terribly scratchy."

Mr Jenkins blinked at Mirabel from behind his jamjar glasses. "There's something about you, Mirabel," he said. "Something I can't quite put my finger on…"

"Please, Mr Jenkins," interrupted Mirabel, "Miss Shirley's class will start in a minute and I don't want to be late on my first day."

"Of course you don't!" said Mr Jenkins. "One thing I will say about you Mirabel is that you're enthusiastic. I think you'll fit into Millbank Juniors very well."

Mirabel prised herself out of the chair. She hoped Mr Jenkins was right about her fitting in. Everything inside the school was half as big as it was at home in the cave.

Chapter 5

Mirabel Meets the Class

Mirabel pushed open the door that said "Class 3C".

"Come in," said Miss Shirley. "Please say, 'Hello, Mirabel,' class."

"Hello, Mirabel," said the class.

"As you're new, I'd like you to tell the class all about yourself," said Miss Shirley.

"I live in some caves near the top of a mountain with my mum," said Mirabel. "We've got a vegetable patch and a nature garden."

Miss Shirley's eyes twinkled. "You must mean you live in a house, Mirabel. A cave would be very chilly in the winter! Now, would anyone in the class like to ask Mirabel a question?"

A boy put his hand in the air.

"Yes, Mohammed?" said Miss Shirley.

"Do you have any pets, Mirabel?" said Mohammed.

"We've got a nanny goat called Blossom," said Mirabel. "We keep her as a pet but we use her for goat's milk and cheese."

"What an unusual pet, and how useful!" said Miss Shirley. "Any more questions, anyone?"

A girl with curly black hair put up her hand.

"Yes, Molly?" said Miss Shirley.

"What flowers do you grow in your garden, Mirabel?" said Molly.

"Ragwort, thistles and stinging nettles," said Mirabel.

The class giggled.

"But those are weeds," said Miss Shirley.

"We grow them to attract bees and insects and nature," said Mirabel.

Miss Shirley clapped her hands together. "Did you hear that, class? How wonderful! I'd love to see your garden one day.

"Sit down now, Mirabel. In the middle of the back row. If I put you in the front, I don't think the others would be able to see the blackboard."

At that moment the door burst open. It was Coral. "Sorry I'm late, Miss Shirley," she panted, "I went to class 3B by mistake."

"Oh, Coral!" sighed Miss Shirley.

"Take a seat next to Mirabel. She's our new girl, sitting in the back row."

Coral grinned at Mirabel. "I've already met her," she said.

Miss Shirley wrote "What I did in my holidays" in curly white letters on the blackboard. "This is what we're all going to write about today," she said.

She gave everyone exercise books and pens. "Write as clearly as you can and we'll all read out what we've written when we've finished."

What I did
in my holidays

Chapter 6

Up in the Tree House

Miss Shirley clapped her hands together. "Time's up, everyone," she said. "As you're new, Mirabel, we'll let you read your story first."

"In the holidays my mum and I decided to help wild animals," began Mirabel. "It's hard for them to find anywhere to make their homes.

Farmers dig up the hedgerows to make way for their crops, and trees are cut down to make way for roads.

"At the end of our garden was a patch of rocky land. Mum and I covered the land with a layer of crumbly, brown earth and planted trees. We watered them every day and the trees grew big and strong.

"We poked holes underneath the trees and planted seeds. Soon, green shoots popped up. They grew and grew and grew. Insects wiggled, birds swooped down and made their nests, and then we called it our nature garden.

"One night the sky was spotty with stars and the moon was like a white fingernail. We climbed up a tree and perched in the tree house we'd built at the top. We listened to frogs croak and crickets sing. A bat got tangled in Mum's beard ... I mean hair," said Mirabel.

"Did it get out again?" asked Mohammed.

"Yes," said Mirabel. "Mum lit her pipe and blew a smoke ring. It frightened the bat away. At midnight we had a picnic. We ate turnip sandwiches with piping hot beetroot juice. Then we heard something creep through the bushes below us. I saw two bright yellow eyes blink up at us from the blackness."

"What was it?" gasped Molly.

YOUNG HIPPO
READERS' CLUB
The sign of good storytelling!

Now you can build your own library of magical, spooky, adventurous and funny Young Hippo tales!

Young Hippo books contain brilliantly written stories by well-known authors, which will stimulate an interest in reading both at home and at school. These highly collectable books are perfect for children who have begun to read full length stories for themselves.

Your introductory pack will be delivered to your home in about 28 days. If for any reason you aren't completely satisfied, just return it to us for a full refund. Then, with no obligation, and for as long as you want, each month we will send you another exciting pack of three books plus a brilliant free gift for only £6.99 (saving pounds on the published price). You can cancel at any time. Send this coupon to the address below with your Parent's/Guardian's signature, with only £4.99 today!

DELIVERED FREE TO YOUR HOME

Your introductory pack will contain: • Whizz Bang and the Crocodile Room • The Wishing Horse • Count Draco Down Under • and a Hippo Glove Puppet

---

☐ Yes! Please send me my introductory Young Hippo Readers' Club pack for only £4.99

THIS SECTION MUST BE COMPLETED BY A PARENT/GUARDIAN

(BLOCK CAPITALS PLEASE)

Parent's/Guardian's name: Mr/Mrs/Ms (Delete as appropriate)

Address

Postcode

Signature

I am over 18

12975–5

Offer valid only in the UK and the Republic of Ireland. If you are not entirely delighted with your introductory offer you can return it for a full refund.

Please make payable to The Red House Ltd. Please return to The Red House Ltd, FREEPOST SCE4316, Windrush Park, Range Road, Witney, OX8 5ZU. (No stamp required).

"It was a fox," said Mirabel. "A fox and her family had come to live in our nature garden. One by one, the fox family crept out of their home. Mum said it was called an earth. We watched the fox cubs wrestle in the moonlight."

For a moment everyone in the class sat very still then Coral jumped up from her chair. "Miss Shirley! Miss Shirley!" she cried. "Can we go on a class outing to visit Mirabel's nature garden? I've only ever seen a bat in a spooky film."

"I'd like to see a fox," said Mohammed.

All the class shouted at once. Miss Shirley clapped her hands together. "What a good idea!" she said. "Will your family mind if the class pay you a visit tomorrow, Mirabel?"

"My mum would love to meet you all," said Mirabel.

"Right!" said Miss Shirley. "Tomorrow I'd like you all to wear comfy trainers. We're going on a class outing to visit Mirabel's nature garden!"

Chapter 7

Fierce, Furry Trolls

The bell rang for breaktime. Everyone tumbled out into the playground. Mohammed started a game of football.

"Come on Mirabel," said Mohammed, as he sped past, dribbling the ball. "You can be in goal, and Coral, you're a great player, you can be in my team."

"I've got something I want to show

Mirabel first," said Coral and grabbed Mirabel's arm. She led her over to a wooden bench and they sat down side by side. Coral pulled a book out of her jacket.

"This is the book about trolls from the class book corner," she said. "I thought I'd better hide it, just in case."

Mirabel peered down at the troll book. It was called *The Blueberry Trolls*. On the cover was a drawing of a troll. It was furry with rather a nasty set of sharp teeth.

"I don't look like that!" said Mirabel. She took the book and flicked over the pages. She read: "Trolls are fierce, furry creatures. They are fearsome, frightening and ferocious. They live at the tops of snowy mountains or in the deepest deserts and darkest forests. No trolls of any kind have been sighted for many years, although on an Arctic expedition, Professor Wilbur Watkins found a large footprint, thought to belong to a Blueberry troll."

Mirabel gave the book back to Coral. "Don't let anyone read that," she said. "Trolls aren't like that at all!"

"What are they like?" said Coral.

"They're gentle and peace loving," replied Mirabel.

"What do you eat?" asked Coral.

"Mostly the vegetables we grow in our vegetable patch," said Mirabel.

"We're experts at gardening and tree climbing. All the animals, birds, fish and insects love us. All the seeds we plant spring up like green fingers, all the trees we climb bend their branches to help us. Mum says they want to do their best for us, because, you see, we're trolls and we look after nature."

Coral tucked the book back inside her jacket. "I wish I was a troll," she sighed. "Will you be my best friend, Mirabel?"

"Yes please!" said Mirabel.

Chapter 8

Mum Gets a Surprise

After school, Mirabel ran all the way back home. She burst into the cave. "Mum! Mum!" she cried. "I've met Mr Jenkins, he's given me a Millbank Juniors jumper. My teacher's called Miss Shirley, she really liked my story, and I've got a new best friend called Coral."

"Well done," said Mum. She prodded a tray of biscuits with a twisty blue fingernail. "Are you hungry, dear?"

"Hmmm, yes," said Mirabel.

"I've got fourteen baked potatoes ready for your tea, I've made you a cabbage crumble as big as the table and I've baked your favourites."

"Sugared trolls?" guessed Mirabel.

Mum grinned. Her beard was covered in crumbs.

A few minutes later, Mirabel had gobbled all the baked potatoes and was tucking into her cabbage crumble. Then she stopped eating, her spoon halfway to her mouth.

"Anything the matter, dear?" said Mum.

"I've just remembered … Miss Shirley's coming to visit," blurted out Mirabel.

Mum spun around, a tray of sugared trolls clattering to the floor. "W-what?" she spluttered. "Mirabel, dear, she'll find out we're trolls!"

"No, she won't," said Mirabel.

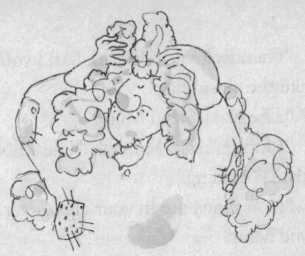

"I'm too big dear, I've got too much hair!" said Mum.

"Don't worry, I'll help," said Mirabel. "You'll have to shave your beard off."

"But I've been growing it since last Christmas," groaned Mum.

"You'll have to comb your hair too," said Mirabel, "and put some make-up on."

Mum plucked a leaf out of her hair and looked at it thoughtfully. "What's Miss Shirley like?" she said.

"Friendly," said Mirabel. "And you'll like the class."

"The class?" said Mum.

"I forgot," said Mirabel. "The whole class is coming."

"How many are in your class, dear?" said Mum.

"Thirty-three," said Mirabel. "Not including Miss Shirley."

"I'll wash the windows and put up new curtains – the old ones are covered in mushrooms. I'll dust the floor and sweep all those cobwebs drooping down from the ceiling," gasped Mum. "I'll have a nice cold bath in the river and put on my best dandelion perfume. When are they coming?"

"Tomorrow morning."

Mum raced to the cupboard and pulled out her broom and feather duster. She charged around the cave, dusting the floor and sweeping the ceiling at the same time.

Mirabel blew a spider off her cabbage crumble.

"I'll find my pretty rosebud dress," puffed Mum. She flung down her feather duster and dashed into her bedroom. She came back holding a small square of material. It was full of holes.

"You can't wear that, Mum," said Mirabel.

"The moths have nibbled it away to almost nothing – it's no bigger than a hanky!" groaned Mum. "I'll have to wear my trousers and you must remind me to take my woolly tights down from the line, I can't have the children seeing those. Hurry up and finish your tea, Mirabel dear. You can help me tidy up."

Chapter 9

A Shock For Miss Shirley

The next morning, the class set off to visit Mirabel's nature garden. At the edge of the city, Miss Shirley counted everybody's heads. "Find a friend to hold hands with," she said.

Coral grabbed Mirabel's hand.

They set off again, until they reached the slatted rope bridge. Coral peered down at the river as it gushed and gurgled over the rocks. "It's a long way down," she said.

"We'll go across in pairs," said Miss Shirley. "Mirabel and Coral can lead the way."

Mirabel and Coral skipped across the bridge followed by the rest of the class.

Miss Shirley and Mohammed came last. Mohammed slipped but grabbed one of Miss Shirley's stringy plaits, just in time. Miss Shirley kept her eyes squeezed tight shut. "Whoooh!" she gasped. "That was fun, wasn't it, everyone? Where to next, Mirabel?"

Mirabel pointed her finger skywards. "Can you see that green smudge at the top of the mountain?"

"My goodness, it is a long way!" said Miss Shirley.

Mirabel led the class, up, up, up the mountainside. The top of the mountain got nearer and nearer. A goat gazed at the class through sleepy yellow eyes. "This is Blossom," said Mirabel, "and this is our nature garden." She pointed at the wild tangle of trees, leaves and weeds.

"It's like a rainforest!" said Mohammed. "Follow me!" Mohammed crashed through the undergrowth like an explorer in the jungle. The nature garden was full of emerald green trees that cast deep, dark shadows.

Sometimes they caught a glimpse of tiny pairs of glittery eyes, blinking out at them from between the leaves.

The class followed along behind Mohammed, then they all popped out the other side.

"We'll all explore the nature garden later," said Mirabel. "First of all you must meet my mum."

The class squelched across the vegetable patch. In front of them loomed the entrance to the cave.

Mirabel's mum strode out. Battered braces held up her trousers. She shook her head and her pirate's earrings rattled. She'd plucked a rose and tucked it behind her ear. She'd shaved off her beard and puffed on her very best pink face powder. As she smiled, her teeth glittered in the sunshine.

Miss Shirley was fumbling inside her handbag. "I'm looking for my diary," she said. "I must jot down the names of some of these wild flowers.

Let's see … ragwort, hedge mustard, wood spurge, fat hen, hogweed…"

"Miss Shirley, this is my mum," said Mirabel.

At that moment, Miss Shirley glanced up at Mum. "Aarggghh!" she screeched. "Run, children!"

But the class had already scattered. Mirabel saw Mohammed's terrified face poke out from behind the apple tree.

"Please don't be frightened," said Mirabel. "I know my mum looks a bit scary, but she'd love to meet you all."

Chapter 10

Adventures in the Nature Garden

"I-I-I'm sorry, I didn't mean to be rude," quavered Miss Shirley.

"It's quite all right," boomed Mum. "Welcome to No. 1, Dragon Haven. My name's Florence Blueberry, but please call me Flo."

"What delightful earrings," gulped Miss Shirley. "Please come out, class, don't hide! Come and say 'Hello' to Flo."

Coral crept out from behind a blackberry bush. "Hello, Flo," she croaked.

Mum bent down, took Coral's hand and gave it a gentle shake. "Pleased to meet you, my dear," she said.

After that, everyone slunk out from their hiding-places. They all queued up to shake Mum by the hand.

"Come into the cave for a bite to eat, my dears," said Mum.

"So, you really do live in a cave, Mirabel!" said Miss Shirley.

Inside the cave, Mum pointed to the table. She'd decorated it with jamjars of stinging nettles surrounded by piles of food. "Tuck in," she said. "I've made turnip sandwiches, cabbage cakes and sugared tr— I mean sugared biscuits. And you can wash it all down with jugs of fresh beetroot juice."

Mum spoke so loudly a few pebbles plopped off the ceiling.

Coral sipped at a jug of beetroot juice, but most of it dribbled down her chin.

Molly nibbled the corner of a cabbage cake, then spat it into her hanky when she thought no one was looking.

Mohammed crunched down half a turnip sandwich. He spluttered and his eyes watered.

"Thank you for making all this lovely food, Flo," said Miss Shirley hastily. "It looks delicious! But if we eat it all, we won't be able to manage our school dinners today."

"What a shame," sighed Mum. Then she gave Mirabel a big wink. "Never mind, my daughter and I will both have enormous suppers tonight!"

"We've come on a school project," explained Miss Shirley. "To visit your nature garden."

"We'll all go outside, my dears," said Mum. "And Mirabel will show you around."

Outside, Mum perched on top of a rock. She lit her pipe and blew large, green smoke rings that drifted over the treetops.

Mirabel led the class back into the nature garden. Juicy green leaves dripped over their heads.

"Will we see any wild animals?" said Coral.

"We'll have to be as quiet as beetles," said Mirabel.

"You find huge, hairy spiders in jungles like this," whispered Coral.

"Good," said Mohammed. "I love spiders!"

Then, high up in a tree, they heard the soft rustle of feathers.

"Can you see her?" said Mirabel. "Right at the top of the tree – it's a blackbird. She's sitting on her nest to keep her eggs warm."

"I can just see the tip of her orange beak," said Molly. "Can we get a closer look?"

Mirabel shook her head. "You can't go too near or you'll frighten her away and her eggs will go cold," she said.

She pointed to a deep hole that tunnelled its way beneath the roots of the tree. "This is the earth where the fox family live."

At that moment, a fox shot out of the earth like a streak of red lightning.

Its white-tipped tail bobbed away through the trees, then it dived behind a bramble bush.

"Wow!" said Mohammed.

"Wicked!" said Coral.

"Crumbs!" said Miss Shirley.

Mirabel led the class further into the nature garden. She stopped and pointed at a crumbly pile of old flower pots. Mohammed peered at them, looking puzzled.

Inside one of the pots, Mirabel showed the class three spiky silver-grey balls.

"What are they?" said Coral. "They look like the things my mum uses to scrub out her saucepans."

"They're a family of hedgehogs," said Mirabel. "They're fast asleep."

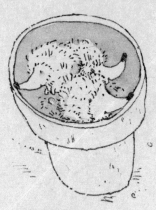

Coral stretched out her fingertips. "Can I stroke them?" she said.

"No," giggled Mirabel. "The grown-up hedgehogs are prickly!"

Miss Shirley glanced at her watch. "My goodness, it's half-past twelve already! Time to hurry back for school dinners."

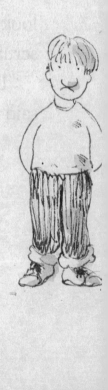

The class groaned.

"Not yet, Miss!" said Mohammed. "Look, there's a big warty thing hiding underneath that log!"

"That's a toad, Mohammed," said Mirabel.

"But I haven't seen any bats or Mirabel's tree house yet!" wailed Coral.

"Please, Miss Shirley, we will come back, won't we?" said Molly.

"We certainly will!" said Miss Shirley.

They wandered back through the trees to the cave. Mum was snoring in the sunshine, her face covered in cabbage cake crumbs and smudges of beetroot juice.

Mirabel tapped her on the shoulder. "Wake up, Mum."

Mum woke up. "I've just finished doing all the washing-up, dear," she lied. "I was totally exhausted!"

"It's time for us all to go back to school, Flo," said Miss Shirley.

Coral gave Mum a kiss goodbye on the cheek. "You're very scratchy," she said.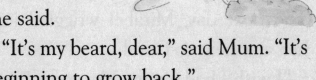

"It's my beard, dear," said Mum. "It's beginning to grow back."

"Ssssh, Mum!" said Mirabel.

The class set off for school. "Goodbye, Flo," they all shouted. "We've all had a lovely time!"

Chapter 11

Coral Gets Stuck

The next day, Mirabel wriggled into her seat next to Coral.

"I wish I had a mum like yours," said Coral.

Miss Shirley tottered into the classroom, balancing a huge pile of books.

"They look heavy," said Mohammed.

"They are!" agreed Miss Shirley. "I've brought them for our book corner. We're all going to start work on nature projects and these books are all about nature."

"Can I do a project about the toad I saw?" said Mohammed.

"Yes," said Miss Shirley, "I've got a book about toads and frogs you can borrow."

"I'll do a project about wild animals," said Coral.

"I'll do one about wild flowers," said Mirabel.

Mirabel found a book on Miss Shirley's desk about wild flowers. "Can I do some of my project outside, Miss Shirley?" she said. "I'll bring wild flower seeds from home and plant them around the edges of the playground and underneath the tree. I'll write about them as they grow."

"Smashing!" said Miss Shirley. "We'll start our own Millbank Juniors nature garden!"

After the class had worked hard on their projects, Miss Shirley clapped her hands together. "Let's all go outside for some fresh air," she said. "We'll have a game. Have you brought your trusty football, Mohammed?"

Mohammed grinned and trotted over to his locker to fetch his football.

Outside in the playground, Miss Shirley blew on the whistle around her neck, and the game began.

"What do I do?" said Mirabel.

Coral pointed at the net. "Kick the

ball into that net and score a goal," she said.

A second later, Mohammed kicked the ball to Mirabel. She squinted at the goalposts. She kicked the ball.

THUMP! The ball whizzed up in the air … and crashed into the highest branches of the tree.

Coral raced across the playground.

"I'll get it!" she cried.

"Come back, Coral!" called Miss Shirley.

But Coral was already scrambling up the tree towards the ball.

The class hurried over to the tree. High up on a branch, perched

Coral. She clung tightly to Mohammed's football.

"Are you all right, Coral?" called Mirabel.

"I'm stuck!" yelled Coral. "I can't get down!"

"Right!" said Miss Shirley. "Don't panic, Coral. Hold tight and don't move."

"I could climb up to her, Miss Shirley," said Mirabel.

"It's all right, Mirabel, we don't want anyone else getting stuck. I'll fetch Mr Jenkins. He's got the key to the caretaker's shed – we'll find a ladder inside."

Miss Shirley scuttled across the playground to Mr Jenkins' office. A moment later, Miss Shirley and Mr Jenkins struggled to heave the ladder out of the caretaker's shed. Mirabel dashed over to help and together they carried the ladder back to the tree.

The rest of the school peered out through their classroom windows to see what was going on, then they all spilled outside and crowded around the tree.

Mr Jenkins propped the ladder up against the tree. He put his foot on the first rung.

"Be careful, Mr Jenkins," said Miss Shirley.

"Don't fuss, April," said Mr Jenkins. "One of my pupils is in danger!"

Mr Jenkins climbed halfway up the ladder, then peered nervously down at the school. "She's very high up," he said. "On second thoughts, we'll have to call for a fireman."

"HELP!" yelled Coral. "I'm stuck like glue! I'm frozen stiff! I can't move, I'm too frightened!"

"Don't worry, Coral, I'm coming to rescue you!" said Mirabel.

"Wait! ... Mirabel!" spluttered Miss Shirley.

But Mirabel was already shinning up the tree trunk. Far above her head, she saw Coral's shiny black shoes and

long white socks. She climbed higher.
The branches seemed to bend towards
her as she climbed.

"Be careful, Mirabel!" called Mr
Jenkins.

The tips of Mirabel's fingers brushed the hem of Coral's skirt. Big, fat tears dripped down Coral's face like crystal tadpoles.

"It's all right, Coral," said Mirabel, softly. "First of all, give me the football."

Coral passed the football to Mirabel and she tucked it down the front of her Millbank Juniors jumper.

"Now climb on to my shoulders," said Mirabel.

"I can't, I'm scared!" croaked Coral.

"Let go bit by bit and grab my hair," said Mirabel.

Coral wriggled on to Mirabel's shoulders and clutched her hair.

"Hold tight!" said Mirabel.

Then she climbed slowly back down the tree with Coral perched on her shoulders. She put Coral safely on the ground and gave Mohammed back his football.

The school burst into claps and cheers.

"Well done, Mirabel!" said Miss Shirley, then she wrapped her jacket around Coral's shoulders. "Are you all right, Coral?"

"Yes, thank you, Miss Shirley," said Coral. "I didn't realize I wouldn't be able to get down again. You see, I wanted to be like Mirabel – Mirabel's a troll."

Coral squashed her hands in front of her mouth, but it was too late.

"A troll!" said Mr Jenkins. "But Mirabel, we don't have trolls at Millbank Juniors!"

Before anyone could say another word, Mirabel ran across the playground, out of the school gates and all the way back home to the cave.

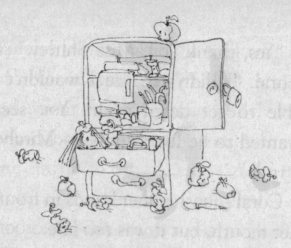

Chapter 12

I Luv Trolls

Early the next morning, Mirabel sneaked back to the school. She'd decided to collect all her things then leave quietly before anyone saw her.

She tiptoed into the classroom and sadly emptied everything out of her locker. She found the book she'd borrowed from Miss Shirley. She'd have to give that back, so she left it on the shelf by the blackboard. She stuffed her exercise books inside her picnic hamper. She also found twelve old apple cores, knots of string and three half-chewed pencils.

She glanced out of the classroom window. Mum was striding across the playground, wearing her best pink hat covered in cherries.

Mirabel hurried outside. "Mum!" she cried. "What are you doing here?"

"I've come to talk to this headteacher of yours, Mr Jenkins. I don't see why he shouldn't let trolls go to Millbank Juniors, dear."

At that moment, Miss Shirley and Mr Jenkins bustled across the playground.

"We saw you both through the staffroom window," said Miss Shirley.

"I've come to have a word with Mr Jenkins," boomed Mum. "He's upset my daughter so much she only managed six helpings of my best cabbage crumble last night!"

"This is Mr Jenkins," said Miss Shirley. "Mr Jenkins, meet Mirabel's mum, Flo."

Mr Jenkins turned pale. "G-g-good morning," he spluttered.

Then, the other side of the school fence, Mirabel saw a long crocodile of children. They stretched all the way down the road and disappeared around the corner. They all spilled through the school gates. At the front of the crocodile was Coral.

She held up a banner. Around the edges she'd drawn lots of blue trolls holding hands. In the middle it said:

I luv trolls!

Mohammed trotted behind Coral. He held up a banner, too. It was covered in flowers made out of tissue paper and milk bottle tops. His banner said:

let Mirabel stay! Trolls have rights too!

The whole school crowded around Mr Jenkins. "We want Mirabel to stay," said Coral. "She saved my life!"

"We had a great time at her nature garden," said Mohammed.

"I got a gold star for my nature project," announced Molly. "I've never had a gold star before!"

"We've all learnt about nature, thanks to Mirabel," added Miss Shirley.

Mr Jenkins paced up and down with a thoughtful look on his face.

"We don't want Mirabel to leave, we're all her friends!" pleaded Coral.

Behind his jamjar glasses, Mr Jenkins' eyes sparkled. His face broke into a big grin. "Well, you've persuaded me!" he said. "I'm going to let Mirabel stay at school!"

Mirabel looked at Mum and Mum gave her a big wink.

The school clapped, cheered and jumped up and down. "Mirabel can stay!" they shouted. "Yippee! Millbank Juniors is a school for trolls!"

The End